D0938329

Bandit's Surprise

by Karen Rostoker-Gruber

illustrated by Vincent Nguyen

Marshall Cavendish Children

Marshall Cavendish Corporation
99 White Plains Road
Tarrytown, NY 10591
www.marshallcavendish.us/kids

Library of Congress Cataloging-in-Publication Data

Rostoker-Gruber, Karen.
Bandit's surprise / by Karen Rostoker-Gruber;
illustrated by Vincent Nguyen. — 1st ed.
p. cm.
Summary: When Michelle brings home a new
kitten, Bandit is not at all pleased to share his
home and water dish, and absolutely refuses to
share his favorite toy mouse.
ISBN 978-0-7614-5623-0
[1. Cats—Fiction. 2. Animals, Infancy—Fiction.]
I. Nguyen, Vincent, ill. II. Title.
PZ7.R72375Bar 2010
[E]—dc22
2009005954

The illustrations are rendered in Graphite pencil,
ink, watercolor, and Photoshop.
Book design by Vera Soki
Editor: Margery Cuyler
Printed in Malaysia (T)
First edition
1 3 5 6 4 2

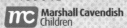

For Emily Nix
—V.N.

Thank you to Bernice Goll, Shawna Lattimore, and their kitten Maya for a purr-fectly wonderful tale. A world of thanks to Dawn Rostoker-Kiron; Ronni Heyman; Andrea Ferreira; my daughter, Michelle; and my husband, Scott, who helped me find the perfect name for the new kitten. And a very special thanks to my father, Earl, and my mother, Marge, who support me whenever times get tough.
—K. R-G.

Bandit paced back and forth.

I wonder what the
surprise is.
A new toy?
A new blanket?
Tasty minced clams?

**Soon Bandit grew tired of
waiting. He curled up in
his favorite sunny spot
and fell asleep.**

When Michelle came home, she set Bandit's carrier down in front of him.

Bandit sniffed the carrier . . .

and walked around it.

Mitzy leaped toward Bandit and pounced on his tail.

Paws off, Purr-brain.

Bandit hissed and ran away. Mitzy ran after him.

Go away, Copycat.

Mitzy drank out of Bandit's
water bowl . . .

ate from Bandit's food bowl . . .

and used Bandit's litter box, but missed.

Mice try, Kitty Litter.

Bandit's ears flattened. He took a swipe at Mitzy's face.

Mitzy ran off.

Mitzy sat in the middle of the floor and meowled.

Bandit leaped through the open window.

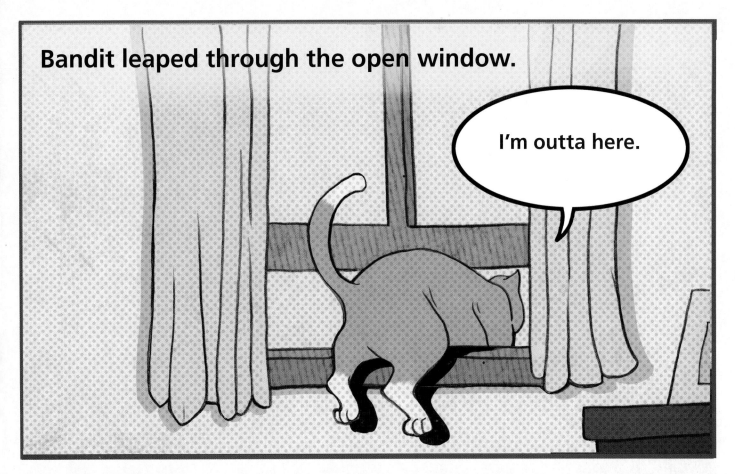

I'm outta here.

He ran and ran and ran.

Then it started to rain.

Bandit ran back to his house.

Michelle picked up Bandit and dried him off.

Watch it, Lady. I'm fragile.

Mitzy play-pounced Bandit's towel.

Stop it, Hair ball.

Time for dinner, you two. It's minced clams.

You don't know what you're missing.

Bandit ate from his food bowl. Mitzy smelled the clams, but turned up her nose.

Bandit drank from his water bowl.

Mitzy drank from Bandit's water bowl, too.

Bandit curled up to Fuzzy Mouse.
Mitzy curled up to Bandit.

Then Mitzy put her paw on Fuzzy
Mouse.